Mark Twain

The £ 1,000,000
Bank Note

百萬英鎊

商務印書館

This Chinese edition of *The £ 1,000,000 Bank Note*
has been published with the written permission of
Black Cat Publishing.

The copyright of this Chinese edition is owned by
The Commercial Press (H.K.) Ltd.

Name of Book: The £ 1,000,000 Bank Note
Author: Mark Twain
Text adaptation, notes and activities: Gina D. B. Clemen
Editors: Rebecca Raynes, Claudia Fiocco
Art direction: Nadia Maestri
Computer graphics realisation: Simona Corniola
Illustrations: Franco Grazioli
Edition: © 2003 Black Cat Publishing
           an imprint of Cideb Editrice, Genoa, Canterbury

系 列 名：Black Cat 優質英語階梯閱讀 · Level 4
書　　名：百萬英鎊
責任編輯：傅　伊
封面設計：張　毅
出　　版：商務印書館（香港）有限公司
　　　　　香港筲箕灣耀興道 3 號東滙廣場 8 樓
　　　　　http://www.commercialpress.com.hk
發　　行：香港聯合書刊物流有限公司
　　　　　香港新界大埔汀麗路 36 號中華商務印刷大廈 3 字樓
印　　刷：中華商務彩色印刷有限公司
　　　　　香港新界大埔汀麗路 36 號中華商務印刷大廈
版　　次：2013 年 5 月第 1 版第 5 次印刷
　　　　　© 商務印書館（香港）有限公司
　　　　　ISBN 978 962 07 1648 5
　　　　　Printed in Hong Kong

出版説明

　　本館一向倡導優質閱讀，近年來連續推出了以 "Q" 為標識的 "Quality English Learning 優質英語學習" 系列，其中《讀名著學英語》叢書，更是香港書展入選好書，讀者反響令人鼓舞。推動社會閱讀風氣，推動英語經典閱讀，藉閱讀拓廣世界視野，提高英語水平，已經成為一種潮流。

　　然良好閱讀習慣的養成非一日之功，大多數初、中級程度的讀者，常視直接閱讀厚重的原著為畏途。如何給年輕的讀者提供切實的指引和幫助，如何既提供優質的學習素材，又提供名師的教學方法，是當下社會關注的重要問題。針對這種情況，本館特別延請香港名校名師，根據多年豐富的教學經驗，精選海外適合初、中級英語程度讀者的優質經典讀物，有系統地出版了這套叢書，名為《Black Cat 優質英語階梯閱讀》。

　　《Black Cat 優質英語階梯閱讀》體現了香港名校名師堅持經典學習的教學理念，以及多年行之有效的學習方法。既有經過改寫和縮寫的經典名著，又有富創意的現代作品；既有精心設計的聽、説、讀、寫綜合練習，又有豐富的歷史文化知識；既有彩色插圖、繪圖和照片，又有英美專業演員朗讀作品的 CD。適合口味不同的讀者享受閱讀之樂，欣賞經典之美。

　　《Black Cat 優質英語階梯閱讀》由淺入深，逐階提升，好像參與一個尋寶遊戲，入門並不難，但要真正尋得寶藏，需要投入，更需要堅持。只有置身其中的人，才能體味純正英語的魅力，領略得到真寶的快樂。當英語閱讀成為自己生活的一部分，英語水平的提高自然水到渠成。

商務印書館（香港）有限公司

編輯部

使用説明 _____

◆1 應該怎樣選書？

按閱讀興趣選書

《Black Cat 優質英語階梯閱讀》精選世界經典作品，也包括富於創意的現代作品；既有膾炙人口的小説、戲劇，又有非小説類的文化知識讀物，品種豐富，內容多樣，適合口味不同的讀者挑選自己感興趣的書，享受閱讀的樂趣。

按英語程度選書

《Black Cat 優質英語階梯閱讀》現設 Level 1 至 Level 6，由淺入深，涵蓋初、中級英語程度。讀物分級採用了國際上通用的劃分標準，主要以詞彙（vocabulary）和結構（structures）劃分。

Level 1 至 Level 3 出現的詞彙較淺顯，相對深的核心詞彙均配上中文解釋，節省讀者查找詞典的時間，以專心理解正文內容。在註釋的幫助下，讀者若能流暢地閱讀正文內容，就不用擔心這一本書程度過深。

Level 1 至 Level 3 出現的動詞時態形式和句子結構比較簡單。動詞時態形式以現在時（present simple）、現在時進行式（present continuous）、過去時（past simple）為主，句子結構大部分是簡單句（simple sentences）。此外，還包括比較級和最高級（comparative and superlative forms）、可數和不可數名詞（countable and uncountable nouns）以及冠詞（articles）等語法知識點。

Level 4 至 Level 6 出現的動詞時態形式，以現在完成時（present perfect）、現在完成時進行式（present perfect continuous）、過去完成時（past perfect continuous）為主，句子結構大部分是複合句（compound sentences）、條件從句（1st and 2nd conditional sentences）等。此外，還包括情態動詞（modal verbs）、被動形式（passive forms）、動名詞（gerunds）、

短語動詞（phrasal verbs）等語法知識點。

根據上述的語法範圍，讀者可按自己實際的英語水平，如詞彙量、語法知識、理解能力、閱讀能力等自主選擇，不再受制於學校年級劃分或學歷高低的約束，完全根據個人需要選擇合適的讀物。

② 怎樣提高閱讀效果？

閱讀的方法主要有兩種：一是泛讀，二是精讀。兩者各有功能，適當地結合使用，相輔相成，有事半功倍之效。

泛讀，指閱讀大量適合自己程度（可稍淺，但不能過深）、不同內容、風格、體裁的讀物，但求明白內容大意，不用花費太多時間鑽研細節，主要作用是多接觸英語，減輕對它的生疏感，鞏固以前所學過的英語，讓腦子在潛意識中吸收詞彙用法、語法結構等。

精讀，指小心認真地閱讀內容精彩、組織有條理、遣詞造句又正確的作品，着重點在於理解"準確"及"深入"，欣賞其精彩獨到之處。精讀時，可充分利用書中精心設計的練習，學習掌握有用的英語詞彙和語法知識。精讀後，可再花十分鐘朗讀其中一小段有趣的文字，邊唸邊細心領會文字的結構和意思。

《Black Cat 優質英語階梯閱讀》中的作品均值得精讀，如時間有限，不妨嘗試每兩個星期泛讀一本，輔以每星期挑選書中一章精彩的文字精讀。要學好英語，持之以恆地泛讀和精讀英文是最有效的方法。

③ 本系列的練習與測試有何功能？

《Black Cat 優質英語階梯閱讀》特別注重練習的設計，為讀者考慮周到，切合實用需求，學習功能強。每章後均配有訓練聽、說、讀、寫四項技能的練習，分量、難度恰到好處。

聽力練習分兩類，一是重聽故事回答問題，二是聆聽主角對話、書信朗讀、或模擬記者訪問後寫出答案，旨在以生活化的練習形式逐步提高聽力。每本書均配有 CD 提供作品朗讀，朗讀者都是專業演員，英國作品由英國演員錄音，美國作品由美國演員錄音，務求增加聆聽的真實感和感染力。多聆聽英式和美式英語兩種發音，可讓讀者熟悉二者的差異，逐漸培養分辨英美發音的能力，提高聆聽理解的準確度。此外，模仿錄音朗讀故事或模仿主人翁在戲劇中的對白，都是訓練口語能力的好方法。

閱讀理解練習形式多樣化，有縱橫字謎、配對、填空、字句重組等等，注重訓練讀者的理解、推敲和聯想等多種閱讀技能。

寫作練習尤具新意，教讀者使用網式圖示（spidergrams）記錄重點，採用問答、書信、電報、記者採訪等多樣化形式，鼓勵讀者動手寫作。

書後更設有升級測試（Exit Test）及答案，供讀者檢查學習效果。充分利用書中的練習和測試，可全面提升聽、說、讀、寫四項技能。

④ 本系列還能提供甚麼幫助？

《Black Cat 優質英語階梯閱讀》提倡豐富多元的現代閱讀，巧用書中提供的資訊，有助於提升英語理解力，擴闊視野。

每本書都設有專章介紹相關的歷史文化知識，經典名著更有作者生平、社會背景等資訊。書內富有表現力的彩色插圖、繪圖和照片，使閱讀充滿趣味，部分加上如何解讀古典名畫的指導，增長見識。有的書還提供一些與主題相關的網址，比如關於不同國家的節慶源流的網址，讓讀者多利用網上資源增進知識。

Contents

T: GRADE 2   Trinity-style exercises (Grade 2)

PET   Cambridge Preliminary English Test-style exercises

This story is recorded in full. 故事錄音

 END   These symbols indicate the beginning and end of the extracts linked to the listening activities. 聽力練習開始和結束的標記

Samuel Langhorne Clemens (1835-1910).
Library of Congress.

A NOTE ON MARK TWAIN

Mark Twain's real name was Samuel Langhorne Clemens. He was born in Florida, Missouri, U.S.A. in 1835. When he was a young boy he lived a happy life in Hannibal, Missouri, on the Mississippi River. In 1857 he worked as a pilot [1] on a steamboat on the Mississippi. He liked traveling on this big river.

After the American Civil War started in 1861, Mark Twain went to California to look for gold. This was the time of the California Gold Rush.

1.   **pilot** : a person who guides a ship along a river into a harbour.

In California, Twain's life changed. He began writing stories for a San Francisco newspaper, and he changed his real name, Samuel Clemens, to Mark Twain, a pen name. [1]

His short story, "The Celebrated Jumping Frog of Calaveras County," was a great success in 1865. Twain was now a famous writer. He traveled to Europe, The Holy Land and Hawaii. He wrote about his travels in *The Innocents Abroad* (1869) and *Roughing It* (1872).

Twain married Olivia "Livy" Langdon, a rich woman from New England, and had three daughters. He lived in Hartford, Connecticut with his family and wrote his three great books, *The Adventures of Tom Sawyer* (1876), *Life on the Mississippi* (1883) and *The Adventures of Huckleberry Finn* (1884). In these books he remembered his youth on the Mississippi River. His other works include *The Prince and the Pauper* (1880), *A Connecticut Yankee in King Arthur's Court* (1889) and many short stories.

At the end of his life, Twain was a very sad man because he lost his wife and two daughters. He died in 1910 at the age of seventy-five.

Mark Twain was the first American writer to change the American way of writing, because he wrote in the vernacular, [2] with his lively [3] humor [4] and satire. [5]

---

1. **pen name** : a name used by a writer instead of his real name.
2. **the vernacular** : the everyday language spoken by the people.
3. **lively** : full of life.
4. **humor** : fun, amusement.
5. **satire** : writing that attacks the faults of society by making fun of them.

SAN FRANCISCO IN THE 1850s

At the beginning of the 1800s, San Francisco, then called Yerba Buena, was a quiet Spanish village. There were a presidio, [1] a Spanish church called Mission Dolores, and some simple homes. There were few ships in the big bay.

With the discovery of gold at Sutter's Fort in 1848, everything changed. San Francisco suddenly grew into a busy city. In only

"Forty-niners". [2]

---

1. **presidio** : Spanish word for military fort.
2. **forty-niners** : gold miners who came to California in 1849.

one year, its population went from 1,000 to 30,000. Settlers came from all over the world. They came to open shops, saloons, hotels, restaurants, banks and trading companies. [1]

There was a population explosion in California. The new settlers needed all types of things from the industries on the East Coast. The sea route [2] from New York to San Francisco became an important one. The port of San Francisco was full of sailing ships.

In the 1850s, at the time of this story, San Francisco was the most important city on the Pacific Coast. The important gold mines in the Sierra Nevada Mountains had their offices in San Francisco. And that is where this story begins.

San Francisco in the 1850s.

1. **trading companies** : companies that buy and sell things.
2. **route** : way.

1 Decide if each sentence is correct or incorrect. If it is correct, tick (✓) A; if it is incorrect, tick (✓) B.

	A	B
1. The old name of San Francisco was Yerba Buena.	☐	☐
2. At the beginning of the 1800s, there were a lot of ships in the big bay.	☐	☐
3. Gold was discovered at Sutter's Fort in 1848.	☐	☐
4. In only one month, its population went from 1,000 to 30,000.	☐	☐
5. Settlers came from all over the world.	☐	☐
6. In the 1850s, San Francisco was the most important city in America.	☐	☐
7. This story begins in the Sierra Nevada Mountains.	☐	☐

2 Now, correct the wrong sentences.

....

....

....

....

....

....

....

Before you read

1 Listen to Part 1 and put the pictures in the order they are mentioned.

a ☐

b ☐

c ☐

d ☐

e ☐

f ☐

From San Francisco to London

 hen I was 27 years old, I worked in an office in San Francisco. I did my job well and my future was promising. [1] I was alone in the world and I was happy.

On Saturday afternoons I didn't work. I sailed my little sailboat [2] on San Francisco Bay. One Saturday afternoon, I sailed out too far. The strong afternoon wind pushed my sailboat out of the bay, into the Pacific Ocean.

---

1. **promising** : (here) favorable.

2. **sailboat** :

That night, when I had lost all hope, a small British brig [1] saw me and took me on board. [2] The brig was sailing to London. The voyage was long and stormy. [3] I worked as a sailor to pay for my trip.

When I arrived in London, my clothes were old and dirty. I had only one dollar in my pocket. With this dollar, I ate and slept for the first twenty-four hours. During the next twenty-four hours, I didn't eat and I didn't sleep.

At about ten o'clock the following morning, I went to Portland Place. I saw a child walking past, holding a big pear. The child ate one small piece and then threw the pear onto the street.

I stopped and looked at it. I was very hungry and I really wanted that pear. But every time I tried to get it, someone passed by and looked at me. I quickly turned in the other direction and waited for the person to pass by. I tried

1. **brig** : sailing ship.
2. **on board** : on a ship.
3. **stormy** : having strong winds and heavy rain.

again and again to get that pear, but the same thing happened. I was desperate. [1] I decided to get the pear and not to worry about the people who saw me. At that moment, a gentleman opened a window behind me and said, "Come in here, please."

A well-dressed servant [2] opened the door. He took me to a beautiful room. Here, two old gentlemen were sitting and discussing something important.

Their breakfast was still on the table. I was very hungry and I stared [3] at their breakfast.

I want to tell the reader that the two gentlemen had made a bet [4] several days before. I knew nothing about the bet until later. Let me tell you what happened.

1. **desperate** : having no hope.
2. **servant** : person who works in a home.
3. **stared** : looked at for a long time with wide-open eyes.
4. **bet** : agreement to risk money on the result of a future event in the hope to win more money.

1 **What happened in Part 1?**

  a. Where did the story begin?

  b. What did the strong wind do to the sailboat?

  c. How did the narrator of the story reach London?

  d. Why did the narrator want the pear?

  e. What were the two old gentlemen doing?

2 **Odd one out!**
Circle the word that doesn't belong to the group.

1. **a.** dinner	**b.** breakfast	**c.** food	**d.** lunch
2. **a.** bread	**b.** pear	**c.** apple	**d.** orange
3. **a.** boat	**b.** bicycle	**c.** ship	**d.** brig
4. **a.** afternoon	**b.** morning	**c.** week	**d.** evening
5. **a.** ocean	**b.** bay	**c.** sea	**d.** river
6. **a.** voyage	**b.** trip	**c.** holiday	**d.** journey

Now write a sentence with each odd word.

  1. ....

  2. ....

  3. ....

  4. ....

  5. ....

  6. ....

SAILING SHIPS

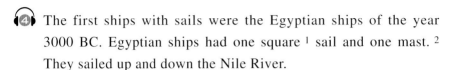

The first ships with sails were the Egyptian ships of the year 3000 BC. Egyptian ships had one square [1] sail and one mast. [2] They sailed up and down the Nile River.

The Roman ships of the year 200 AD had one square sail, with a topsail [3] above it. In front of the ship there was a foresail. [4] The Roman ships had only one mast.

The Vikings from the north also had ships with one square sail and one mast.

The Egyptians, the Romans and the Vikings all used oars [5] to guide their ships.

The first sailing ships with two or more masts came from China. Marco Polo, the Italian merchant and traveler, brought this new idea from China to Italy in 1295.

Between the years 1400 and 1600, sailing ships changed a lot.

By the end of the 1400s, ships with three masts were common in Europe.

After the 1750s, European sailing ships had from two to six masts. Different types of ships had different names: the caravel, the carrack, the galleon, the schooner, the brig, the brigantine. These ships sailed all over the world.

The new clipper sailing ship was very fast and light. It sailed at great speed. In 1854 the clipper ship, *Flying Cloud*, traveled

1. **square** : having four equal sides and four right angles.
2. **mast** →
3. **topsail**

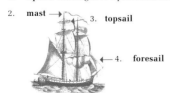

←— 4. **foresail**

5. **oars** :

from New York to San Francisco in only 89 days and 8 hours. This was half the time of other ships.

During the California Gold Rush in the 1850s and 1860s, thousands of people traveled on clippers from New York to San Francisco. From San Francisco, these people went to the California Gold Country to look for gold.

The English brig, that took the narrator [1] of the story to London, had two masts and two large, square sails.

The Clipper Ship *Red Jacket*, 1854, from a Currier and Ives print.

1. **narrator** : person who tells a story.

1 **Choose the correct answer.**

a. The first ships with sails were the
- [ ] Roman ships
- [ ] Egyptian ships
- [ ] caravels

b. To guide their sailing ships, the Egyptians and the Romans used
- [ ] a square sail
- [ ] a mast
- [ ] oars

c. The first sailing ships with two or more masts came from
- [ ] Italy
- [ ] China
- [ ] Egypt

d. The fastest sailing ship was the
- [ ] clipper
- [ ] brig
- [ ] brigantine

e. In the 1850s and 1860s, thousands of people traveled on clipper ships to reach
- [ ] New York
- [ ] San Francisco
- [ ] London

f. The narrator of the story traveled to London on a
- [ ] clipper
- [ ] schooner
- [ ] brig

SAILING ON SAN FRANCISCO BAY

Sailing on San Francisco Bay was popular in the 1800s and it still is today. There is always a lot of wind in San Francisco and this is perfect for sailing and windsurfing. [1] The wind usually comes from the West and the North West. [2] The west wind is a strong wind, but it is not cold.

When the wind is very strong, it can push small sailboats out of the bay and into the Pacific Ocean.

Sailing in San Francisco Bay.

1. **windsurfing** : the sport of moving over water on a special board with a sail.

2. **West and the North West** :

A shark.

The waters of San Francisco Bay are cold all year. Their temperature in the summer is between 10° and 13° C. Sharks often swim in the bay.

There are a lot of exciting regattas [1] on the bay. When there is an important regatta, there are hundreds of sailboats with colorful sails.

In San Francisco, the sailing season begins the last Sunday of April, and finishes at the end of October.

Forty kilometers outside San Francisco Bay, in the Pacific Ocean, there are the Farallon Islands. Here, there is a marine [2] sanctuary; [3] a protected place where fish, whales, [4] seals [5] and rare birds live.

In winter and in spring, gray whales visit the Farallon Islands. In autumn, the huge blue whale swims past these islands.

Outside San Francisco Bay, there is another marine sanctuary called Point Reyes Peninsula. Seals and rare birds live on this beautiful peninsula.

1. **regattas** : sporting events at which races are held between rowing-boats or yachts.

2. **marine** : of the sea.

3. **sanctuary** : area where birds and wild animals are protected from hunters and are encouraged to breed.

4. **whales** :

5. **seals** :

1 Match the correct parts of the sentences.

a.	The wind usually comes	**1.**	in autumn.
b.	The west wind is strong	**2.**	are cold all year.
c.	The waters of San Francisco Bay	**3.**	in spring.
d.	The sailing season begins	**4.**	a marine sanctuary.
e.	The Farallon Islands are	**5.**	from the West and North West.
f.	Huge blue whales swim past	**6.**	but not cold.

2 Can you find the hidden names of the four animals that live in the Farallon Island Marine Sanctuary?

R	W	P	O	S	G	F	E	I
S	Z	H	R	B	I	R	D	S
E	C	B	A	T	U	V	G	J
A	N	T	M	L	F	C	W	K
L	J	H	V	Q	E	N	F	M
S	T	D	C	F	I	S	H	Y
C	A	S	T	F	O	G	W	N

....

....

INTERNET PROJECT

In California there are two exceptional aquariums: [1] the Steinhart Aquarium, the oldest aquarium in the United States, and the Monterey Bay Aquarium, one of the newest American aquariums.

LET'S VISIT THEIR WEBSITES!
1. Visit the **Steinhart Aquarium** and the **Monterey Bay Aquarium**.
2. Write a short report about them.

The Steinhart Aquarium

In San Francisco the Steinhart Aquarium is a very important sea life center with 6,000 different types of sea animals. In this beautiful aquarium you can see tropical sharks, a colony of black-footed penguins, reptiles, alligators and other amphibians. [2]

You can find out about:

- the coral reef and the fish
- the sharks
- the penguin colony
- the seahorses
- the reptiles and amphibians

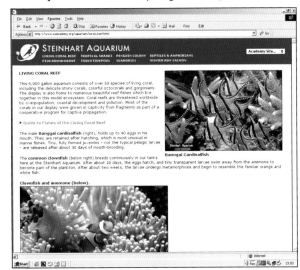

---

1. **aquariums** : buildings containing many fish and other water animals.

2. **amphibians** : animals able to live both on land and in water.

The Monterey Bay Aquarium

The Monterey Bay Aquarium is located in Monterey, a city south of San Francisco. It was built on Monterey Bay. The aquarium opened in 1984 and about 300,000 sea animals and plants live there. It is one of the most modern and well-equipped [1] aquariums in the world.

You can find out about:

- sea otters [2]

- octopuses [3]

- marine mammals
  (seals and whales)

- penguins

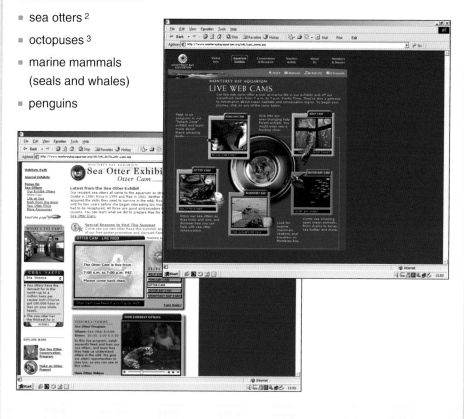

1. **well-equipped** : with all the things needed.
2. **otters** : small fish-eating river animals.
3. **octopuses** : sea-animals with eight arms.

Before you read

PET

1 Listen to the first part of Part 2. Then choose the correct answer.

1. The two old gentlemen were
   A ☐ good friends
   B ☐ brothers
   C ☐ cousins

2. They decided to end their argument with
   A ☐ a strange promise
   B ☐ a cup of tea
   C ☐ a bet

3. The Bank of England issued two banknotes of
   A ☐ a million pounds each
   B ☐ half a million pounds each
   C ☐ eight million pounds each

4. The Bank of England issued the banknotes
   A ☐ to pay a debt with a foreign country
   B ☐ for a private transaction
   C ☐ for a public transaction with a foreign country

5. Brother A thought that if a stranger arrived in London without money, except for the £ 1,000,000 banknote
   A ☐ he would spend it all
   B ☐ he would starve to death
   C ☐ he would be very happy

6. Brother A thought that if he went to the bank to change the big note, the police would
   A ☐ help him find the owner of the note
   B ☐ ask him many questions
   C ☐ put him in prison

PART 2

An Unusual Bet

T he two old gentlemen were brothers. For several days, they argued [1] about a very strange subject. They decided to end their argument with a bet, as the English usually do. The following was the subject of the bet.

The Bank of England issued two banknotes of a million pounds each for a public transaction [2] with a foreign country. England used one banknote and the other remained in the bank.

At this point, Brother A said to Brother B, "If an honest and

---

1. **argued** : discussed.
2. **transaction** : business.

intelligent stranger arrives in London without a friend and without money, except for the £ 1,000,000 banknote, he will starve to death." [1]

Brother B answered, "No! I don't agree."

Brother A said, "If he goes to the bank or anywhere else to change this big note, the police will put him in prison. END Everyone will think he stole [2] it."

1. **starve to death** : die from lack of food.
2. **stole** : took what belongs to another person (to steal - stole - stolen).

They continued arguing for days, until Brother B said, "I'll bet £ 20,000 that the stranger will live for thirty days with the banknote and not go to prison."

Brother A accepted the bet. He went to the bank and bought the £ 1,000,000 banknote. After, he returned home and prepared a letter. Then the two brothers sat by [1] the window and waited for the right man for the bet.

They saw a lot of honest faces go by, but they were not intelligent enough. Several faces were intelligent, but they were not honest. A lot of faces were honest and intelligent, but they were not poor enough. [2] Other faces were honest, intelligent and poor, but they were not strangers.

When they saw me from the window, they thought I was the right man. They asked me questions, and soon they knew my story. Finally, they told me I was the right man for the bet. I asked them to explain the bet. One of the gentlemen gave me an envelope. I wanted to open it, but he said, "No, don't open it now. Wait until you are in your hotel room. Then read it very carefully."

I was confused and I wanted to discuss the subject with them. But they didn't. I felt hurt [3] because I was the subject of a joke. [4]

When I left their house, I looked for the pear on the street. It was gone. I was quite angry with those two gentlemen.

1. **by** : very near.
2. **poor enough** : sufficiently poor.
3. **hurt** : (here) offended.
4. **subject of a joke** : made to look silly.

Far from their house, I opened the envelope. I saw that there was money inside! I didn't stop to read their letter.

I ran to the nearest eating place. I ate and ate and ate. At last, I took out the envelope with the money, to pay for my meal. I looked at the banknote and almost fainted. [1] It was a banknote worth [2] five million dollars!

I was speechless. [3] I stared at the banknote. The two gentlemen had made a big mistake. They probably wanted to give me a one-pound banknote.

I saw the owner of the eating place staring at the banknote, too. We were both surprised. I did not know what to do or say. So, I simply [4] gave him the note and said, "Give me the change, please."

The owner apologized [5] a thousand times.

"I'm very sorry, but I can't change this banknote, sir."

---

1. **fainted** : lost consciousness.
2. **worth** : with the value of.
3. **speechless** : not able to speak.
4. **simply** : only.
5. **apologized** : said he was sorry.

"I don't have any other money. Please change this note."

The owner then said, "You can pay for this food whenever you want, sir. I understand that you are a very rich gentleman. You like playing jokes on people by dressing like a poor man. You can come here and eat all you want, whenever you want. You can pay me when you want."

1 **What happened in Part 2?**

a. What did Brother A say to Brother B? Did Brother B agree?

b. What was the subject of the bet?

c. How much money did Brother B bet?

d. Why was the narrator of the story the right man for the bet?

e. What was inside the envelope?

f. Why did the owner of the eating place apologize?

2 **The Past Simple is often used to write a story. Here's a crossword puzzle for you to do.**

What's the Past Simple of:

Down

1. do   **2.** make   **4.** give
5. leave   **8.** go   **9.** see
12. tell

Across

3. say   **6.** argue   **7.** feel
10. are   **11.** steal   **13.** run
14. take

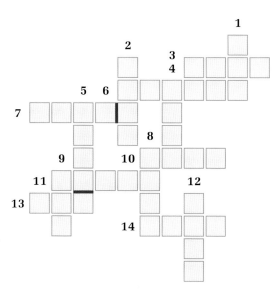

"If clauses"

3 **In Part 2, Brother A said to Brother B:**

If *an honest and intelligent stranger* **arrives** *in London without a friend and without money, except for the £ 1,000,000 banknote, he* **will** *starve to death.*

We use "if clauses" (first conditional（第一類條件分句）) to talk about a possible future situation and its results.

if + Present Simple + will

Look at the example and complete the following sentences.

If he .... *(go)* to the bank, the police .... *(arrest)* him.

If he .*goes*........ to the bank, the police *will arrest*. him.

a. If he .... *(be)* honest and intelligent, he .... *(be)* the right man for the bet.

b. If it .... *(rain)*, we .... *(not go)* to the park.

c. If he .... *(open)* the envelope, he .... *(find)* a letter.

d. I .... *(win)* the bet if I .... *(follow)* the instructions.

e. The wind .... *(push)* me out of the bay if I .... *(sail)* out too far.

f. Their future .... *(be)* promising if they .... *(work)* hard.

THE ENGLISH AND BETTING

 Betting on things that will happen is common in Great Britain. The British love betting. They bet on horse races, dog races, football matches, cricket [1] matches, hockey [2] matches, polo [3] matches and other sports. They also play the lottery. [4]

A lot of betting is very informal. It takes place at the pub. The sum of money that is bet can be small, or very large, depending on the bet.

The famous novel by Jules Verne, *Around the World in Eighty Days*, is the story of an English gentleman who made a big bet. He bet that he could go around the world in eighty days, and then return to his club in London, at a specific time and day.

There are other forms of betting called gambling, where you play cards or other games for money.

Las Vegas, Nevada.

In the United States, an entire city was built for people who like gambling. It's called Las Vegas. The city of Las Vegas, in the state of Nevada, has thousands of places where people can gamble small sums and big ones.

---

1. **cricket** : a game in which players hit a small hard ball with bats.
2. **hockey** : a game in which players hit a small ball with long curved sticks.
3. **polo** : a game in which players on horseback hit a ball with long-handled hammers.
4. **lottery** : a drawing of lots in which prizes are given to winners among persons buying a chance.

PET

1 Decide if each sentence is correct or incorrect. If it is correct, tick (✓) A; if it is incorrect, tick (✓) B.

	A	B
a. The British dislike betting on things.	☐	☐
b. They play the lottery.	☐	☐
c. It is not possible to bet at the pub.	☐	☐
d. *Around the World in Eighty Days* is the story of an important bet.	☐	☐
e. Playing cards for money is called gambling.	☐	☐
f. Las Vegas is a town in the state of California.	☐	☐

2 Think about the questions and write your answers.

a. Are you a lucky person?

Yes ☐   No ☐

b. Do you bet on things?

Yes ☐   No ☐

If not, why not?

....

....

....

c. What do people bet on?

....

....

....

d. Describe an unusual bet you or somebody else made in the past.

....

....

Before you read

PET

1 Listen to Part 3. Decide if each sentence is correct or incorrect. If it is correct, put a tick (✓) in the box under A for YES. If it is not correct, put a tick (✓) in the box under B for NO.

	A YES	B NO
1. The narrator left the eating place and walked slowly to the house of the two gentlemen.	☐	☐
2. The two gentlemen went to Egypt.	☐	☐
3. They will return in a month.	☐	☐
4. The family went to the Continent.	☐	☐
5. There were two signatures on the letter.	☐	☐
6. The two old gentlemen were playing a game.	☐	☐
7. The narrator didn't know anything about the details of the bet.	☐	☐
8. The narrator decided to keep the bill for a whole year.	☐	☐
9. The idea of an important job made the narrator happy.	☐	☐

PART 3

The Letter

hen I left the eating place, I hurried [1] to the house of the two gentlemen. I wanted to correct the mistake they had made. I was very nervous.

When I arrived, the same servant opened the door. I asked for the two gentlemen.

"They are gone," the servant said.

"Gone? Gone where?"

"Oh, on a journey."

"But, where did they go?"

"To the Continent, [2] I think."

"The Continent?"

---

1. **hurried** : went quickly.

2. **Continent** : mainland Europe.

"Yes, sir."

"When will they return?"

"In a month."

"A month! Oh, this is awful! [1] How can I talk to them? It's extremely important."

"I can't help you. I don't know where they are, sir."

"Then I must see a member of the family."

"All the family are away. They're in Egypt and India, I think."

"Before leaving, the two gentlemen made an enormous mistake. They will certainly return home tonight. Tell them that I came here to correct the mistake. I will return tomorrow."

"I'll tell them if I see them. But I won't see them! Sir, you must not worry because everything is all right. They will be here on time, [2] and they will see you then. Good-bye."

I was confused. My head was in a fog. [3] I did not understand what the servant told me. The letter — I remembered the letter! This is what it said:

You are an intelligent and honest man. You are also poor and a stranger. In this envelope you will find some money. It is yours only for 30 days. At the end of 30 days, return to this house. I have a bet on you. If I win this bet, you can have any job with any salary that you want.

---

1. **awful** : terrible.
2. **on time** : not late or early.
3. **in a fog** : puzzled and confused.

There were no signature, [1] no address, no date on the letter.

How strange! I didn't know what to think. I went to a park, sat down and thought about what to do. After an hour, I reached the decision that follows.

The two old gentlemen are playing a game that I don't understand. They are betting on me. (But, at that time, I didn't know anything about the details of the bet.)

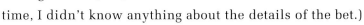

If I go to the Bank of England to return the banknote, the bank will ask me lots of questions. If I tell the truth, no one will believe me. They will put me in an asylum. [2] If I tell a lie, the police will put me in prison. I can't even give it to anyone, because no honest person will want it.

I can do only one thing: I must keep the bill [3] for a whole month. And, I must not lose it. If I help the old man to win his bet, he will give me the job I want.

The idea of an important job with a big salary made me happy. With this exciting idea in mind, I began walking down the streets of London.

---

1. **signature** : a person's name written by himself/herself.

2. **asylum** : mental hospital.
3. **bill** : (here) banknote.

1 What happened in Part 3?

a. Why did the narrator hurry to the house of the two gentlemen?

b. Where did the two gentlemen go?

c. What did the letter say?

d. Why didn't the narrator return the banknote to the Bank of England?

e. What did the narrator plan to do?

f. Which idea made him happy?

PET **2** You are the narrator and you want to write a letter to your best friend in San Francisco. You want to describe what is happening to you in London. Write your letter in about 100 words.

Dear Tom, ...

....

....

....

....

....

....

3 **In Part 3, we see this sentence:**

*I **must** keep the bill for a whole month. And, I **must** not lose it.*

We use **must** and **mustn't** to talk about obligation and necessity, in the present and future.

Look at these pictures and make a sentence describing the message of the picture, using *must* or *mustn't*.

a. ....

b. ....

c. ....

d. ....

e. ....

f. ....

g. ....

LONDINIUM

The Romans founded London almost 2000 years ago on the River Thames. They named it Londinium, and it was part of the province called Britannia. The Romans always founded their colonies near a river. The Roman historian Tacitus wrote that Londinium was a busy center for trade [1] and traders. The geographic [2] position of Londinium, on the river and near the sea, was perfect for trade.

London was almost destroyed by the plague [3] in 1665, and by fire in 1666. In the 19th century, people began moving from the center to the outer parts. [4]

London in the 1600s, by Claude de Jongh.

1. **trade** : buying, selling, exchanging things.
2. **geographic** : of the physical features of a place.
3. **plague** : an infectious, usually fatal disease.
4. **outer parts** : the edges of the city.

Old Londinium is now the part of London called the City, a small area on the north bank of the River Thames. The City is the principal [1] banking and commercial center of Europe. There are more than 500 foreign banks and hundreds of financial companies in this area.

In the City there is still a part of an old Roman wall, and the remains [2] of medieval London. The City has its own cathedral, St Paul's, and its own arts center, the Barbican. There is also an excellent museum, the Museum of London. This museum presents London's history from Roman times.

St Paul's Cathedral.

1. **principal** : main.
2. **remains** : what is left when most of something has gone.

A MAP OF THE CENTER OF LONDON

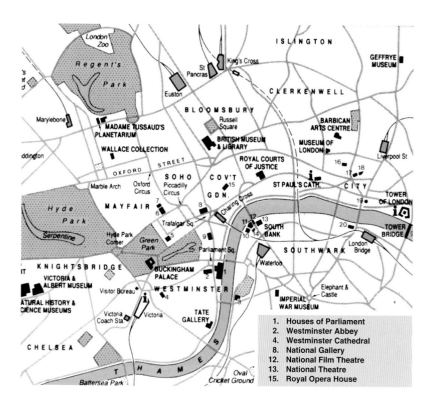

1. Houses of Parliament
2. Westminster Abbey
4. Westminster Cathedral
8. National Gallery
12. National Film Theatre
13. National Theatre
15. Royal Opera House

1 Look at the map of the center of London. Can you find some of the places we've talked about in the City?

a. Which ones? ....

b. How many parks can you count on the map? ....

c. How many museums can you count? ....

d. How many theaters can you count? ....

e. What's the name of the lake in Hyde Park? ....

Before you read

PET

1 Listen to the first part of Part 4, and then put a tick (✓) next to the correct answer.

1. The narrator wanted
   - A ☐ to use the £ 1,000,000 note
   - B ☐ to talk to the tailor
   - C ☐ to buy some new clothes

2. He passed in front of the tailor's
   - A ☐ six times
   - B ☐ sixteen times
   - C ☐ sixty times

3. He quietly asked if they had
   - A ☐ an elegant suit
   - B ☐ an old, unattractive suit
   - C ☐ new clothes

4. A man took him to
   - A ☐ the back room
   - B ☐ the back of the shop
   - C ☐ a black room

5. When it was time to pay, the narrator
   - A ☐ didn't have the £ 1,000,000 note
   - B ☐ didn't have any small change
   - C ☐ decided not to buy the suit

6. The narrator asked if he could pay
   - A ☐ in a month
   - B ☐ in a week
   - C ☐ in a few days

PART 4

At the Tailor's

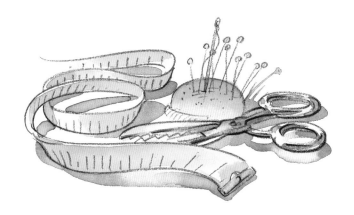

Every time I passed in front of a tailor's, [1] I wanted to enter and buy some new clothes. But, I had no money to pay for them. The £ 1,000,000 banknote in my pocket was useless! [2]

I passed in front of the same tailor's six times. At last I entered. I quietly asked if they had an old, unattractive [3] suit that no one wanted to buy. The man I spoke to nodded [4] his head, but he didn't speak. Then another man looked at me and nodded his head. I went to him and he said, "One moment, please."

1. **tailor's** : shop that makes clothes for men.
2. **useless** : not good for anything.
3. **unattractive** : not pleasing or interesting.
4. **nodded** : moved his head up and down in agreement.

After some time, he took me to a back room. He looked at several ugly suits that no one wanted. He chose the worst for me. I really wanted a suit, so I said nothing.

It was time to pay. "Can you wait a few days for the money? I haven't got any small change [1] with me."

ᴇɴᴅ

The man said, "Oh, you haven't? Well, I thought gentlemen like you carried large change."

"My friend," I replied, "you can't judge a stranger by the clothes he wears. I can pay for this suit. But, can you change a large banknote?"

"Oh, of course we can change a large banknote," he said coldly.

I gave him the banknote. He received it with a smile, a big smile that covered his face. When he read the banknote, his smile disappeared. The owner of the shop came over and asked me, "What's the trouble?" [2]

"There isn't any trouble. I'm waiting for my change."

"Come, come. Give him his change, Tod. Quickly!"

Tod answered, "It's easy to say, but look at the banknote."

The owner looked at the banknote. Then he looked at my package [3] with the ugly suit.

"Tod," he shouted, "you are stupid! How can you sell this unattractive suit to a millionaire! Tod, you can't see the difference between a millionaire [4] and a poor man."

"I apologize, sir," the owner continued. "Please take off those things you are wearing and throw them in the fire. Put on this fine shirt and this handsome suit. It's perfect for you — simple but elegant." [5]

1. **change** : (here) small banknotes, coins.
2. **trouble** : problem.
3. **package** : something that is wrapped in paper.
4. **millionaire** : a very rich person.
5. **elegant** : with a beautiful style.

I told him I was very happy with the new suit.

"Oh, wait until you see what we can make for you in your size! Tod, bring a pen and a book. Let me measure [1] your leg, your arm..."

I didn't have a moment to speak.

The owner measured me. Then he ordered his tailors to make me morning suits, evening suits, shirts, coats and other things.

"But, my dear sir," I said, "I can order all these things *only* if you change my banknote. Or, if you can wait a while [2] before I pay you."

"Wait *a while*! I'll wait *forever*, that's the word. Tod, send these things to the gentleman's address. Let the less important customers [3] wait!

What's your address, sir?"

---

1. **measure** : find the size of somebody.
2. **a while** : a period of time.
3. **customers** : clients, people who buy from a shop.

"I'm changing my home. I'll come back and give you my new address," I replied.

"Quite right, sir, quite right. Let me show you to the door, sir. Good day, sir, good day."

PET **1** **Read the text below and choose the correct word for each space. For each question, write the correct letter A, B, C or D. The first one is done for you.**

I wanted new (1) .B.. but I had (2) ..... money. No one could (3) ..... the million pound banknote. I went to the tailor's and he (4) ..... the worst suit for me. When I showed him my banknote (5) ..... changed. The owner of the shop said, "He's a millionaire!"

He gave me (6) ..... fine clothes and ordered (7) ..... tailors to (8) ..... new suits and coats for me. Everyone was very (9) ..... to me.

1. **A** costumes	**B** clothes	**C** dresses	**D** cloth
2. **A** no	**B** not	**C** none	**D** any
3. **A** have	**B** buy	**C** change	**D** pay
4. **A** chooses	**B** chosen	**C** choose	**D** chose
5. **A** anything	**B** everything	**C** nothing	**D** some
6. **A** none	**B** few	**C** some	**D** any
7. **A** his	**B** him	**C** their	**D** my
8. **A** construct	**B** build	**C** make	**D** do
9. **A** kind	**B** happy	**C** nervous	**D** serious

2 **Match the following words with their opposites.**

a. ugly	**1.** more
b. right	**2.** best
c. less	**3.** small
d. happy	**4.** wrong
e. worst	**5.** easy
f. difficult	**6.** useful
g. large	**7.** beautiful
h. useless	**8.** sad

3 Look at this sentence from Part 4:

*The blue suit was **worse** than the brown one.* (*worse* is a comparative
（比較級）)*He chose **the worst** for me.* (*worst* is a superlative （最高
級）)

Some forms are irregular:

ADJECTIVE	COMPARATIVE	SUPERLATIVE
good	better	best
bad	worse	worst

With one-syllable adjectives （單音節形容詞）**, we add -er for the
comparative form, and -est for the superlative form.**

ADJECTIVE	COMPARATIVE	SUPERLATIVE
cold	colder	coldest
young	younger	youngest

**Fill in the gaps with the correct form of either the comparative
or superlative.**

a. Tod was .... *(poor)* than the shop owner.
The narrator was the .... person in the shop.

b. The west wind was cold, but the east wind was
.... The north wind was the ....

c. This cloak is .... *(cheap)* than the coat. But the
mantel is the .... of all.

d. Brother A was .... *(happy)* than Brother B, but
the narrator was the ....

e. The shop owner was .... *(kind)* than Tod. Harris
was the .... of all.

f. The servant had a big lunch. Brother A had a .... lunch
than Brother B. But the narrator had the .... lunch
of all.

HOW DID PEOPLE DRESS IN THE 1850s?

Clothes during this period were quite elegant. Men wore top hats, elaborate [1] shirts, vests, [2] jackets and coats. Some wore big cloaks. [3] Women wore elaborate dresses, with long skirts. They also wore fashionable [4] hats and bonnets, [5] and mantles. [6]

Women of the 1850's always wore gloves and carried a small umbrella, called a parasol. This parasol protected them from the sun.

The Railway Station, 1862 by William Powell Firth.
Royal Holloway and Bedford New College, Surrey, UK.

1. **elaborate** : carefully prepared and finished.

2. **vest** :

3. **cloak** : long outer clothing without sleeves, shoulders or arms.

4. **fashionable** : following a style that is currently popular.

5. **bonnet** :

6. **mantle** : a short cloak.

1 Can you find seven hidden names of clothing worn in the 1850s? Look at the definitions of the words to help you.

- it protects you from the sun
- a piece of clothing without arms usually worn under a jacket
- a mantle worn over the shoulders
- you wear it on your head to give protection from the weather
- a hat worn by women with ribbons to tie under the chin
- it is like a cloak
- you wear them on your hands

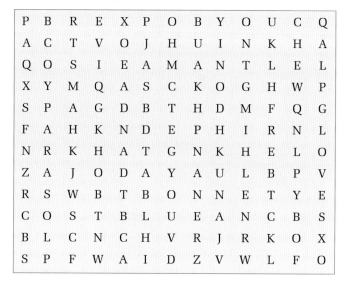

P	B	R	E	X	P	O	B	Y	O	U	C	Q
A	C	T	V	O	J	H	U	I	N	K	H	A
Q	O	S	I	E	A	M	A	N	T	L	E	L
X	Y	M	Q	A	S	C	K	O	G	H	W	P
S	P	A	G	D	B	T	H	D	M	F	Q	G
F	A	H	K	N	D	E	P	H	I	R	N	L
N	R	K	H	A	T	G	N	K	H	E	L	O
Z	A	J	O	D	A	Y	A	U	L	B	P	V
R	S	W	B	T	B	O	N	N	E	T	Y	E
C	O	S	T	B	L	U	E	A	N	C	B	S
B	L	C	N	C	H	V	R	J	R	K	O	X
S	P	F	W	A	I	D	Z	V	W	L	F	O

T: GRADE 2

2 Topic – Clothes
Find in your home an item of clothing which is special or particular to you and think about these questions:

a. Where did it come from? (a gift or inherited or bought)

b. What would it be worn with?

c. Why is it special or particular?

Before you read

PET

1 Listen to Part 5. Decide if each sentence is correct or incorrect. If it is correct, put a tick (✓) in the box under A for YES. If it is not correct, put a tick (✓) in the box under B for NO.

	A YES	B NO
1. The narrator bought everything without money.	☐	☐
2. Only one person was able to change the banknote.	☐	☐
3. The narrator stayed at the Hancock Hotel.	☐	☐
4. He always had dinner at the hotel.	☐	☐
5. He preferred having lunch at Harris's simple eating place.	☐	☐
6. Harris was happy with his new customers.	☐	☐
7. The narrator lived like a rich, important man.	☐	☐
8. People followed the narrator in the streets of London.	☐	☐
9. He never wore his old clothes again.	☐	☐
10. The American Ambassador knew the narrator's grandfather from Yale University.	☐	☐

PART 5

The Poor Millionaire

he impossible happened. I bought everything I wanted without money. I showed my banknote and asked for change, but every time the same thing happened. No one was able to change it.

I bought all that I needed and all the luxuries [1] that I wanted. I stayed at an expensive hotel in Hanover Square. I always had dinner at the hotel. But I preferred having breakfast at Harris's simple eating place. Harris's was the first place where I had a good meal with my million-pound note. That's where it all started.

The news about me and my banknote was all over London.

---

1. **luxuries** : costly things that aren't necessary.

Harris's eating place became famous because I had breakfast there. Harris was happy with all his new customers.

I lived like a rich, important man. I had money to spend. I lived in a dream. But often, I said to myself, "Remember, this dream will end when the two men return to London. Everything will change."

My story was in the newspapers. Everyone talked about the "strange millionaire with the million-pound note in his pocket." *Punch* magazine drew a funny picture of me on the front page. People talked about everything I did and about everything I said. They followed me in the streets.

I kept my old clothes, and sometimes I wore them. It was fun when the shop owners thought I was poor. Then I showed them the banknote, and, oh, how their faces changed!

After ten days in London, I went to visit the American

Ambassador. [1] He was very happy to meet me. He invited me to a dinner-party that evening. He told me that he knew my father from Yale University. He invited me to visit his home whenever I wanted.

I was glad to have a new, important friend. I thought to myself, "I'll need an important friend, when the story of the million-pound note and bet comes out." [2]

I want the reader to know that I planned to pay back all the shop owners who sold me things on credit. [3] "If I win the bet for the old gentleman," I thought, "I will have an important job. With an important job, I will have a big salary." I planned to pay back everyone with my first year's salary.

END

1. **ambassador** : an important person who is the official representative of his/her country in another country.
2. **comes out** : becomes known.
3. **credit** : buying something and paying for it later.

PET **1** **Read the sentences below. For each question put a tick (✓) in the correct box.**

1. What did the narrator buy with the banknote?
    A ☐ expensive clothes
    B ☐ a hotel in London
    C ☐ only good food
    D ☐ everything he wanted

2. Where did he always have dinner?
    A ☐ at the Ambassador's house
    B ☐ at Harris's eating place
    C ☐ at the hotel in Hanover Square
    D ☐ at Yale University

3. *Punch* magazine
    A ☐ wrote a story about the banknote
    B ☐ drew a funny picture of the narrator on the front page
    C ☐ sent the narrator a gift
    D ☐ wrote a story about San Francisco

4. The American Ambassador
    A ☐ did not want to meet the narrator
    B ☐ knew the two old gentlemen
    C ☐ knew the narrator's brother
    D ☐ invited the narrator to a dinner party

5. With his first year's salary the narrator
    A ☐ planned to buy a big home
    B ☐ planned to pay back all the shop owners
    C ☐ planned to make a big bet
    D ☐ planned to buy Harris's eating place

2 Put the jumbled letters in correct order to form a word. Then match the word to its meaning.

a. esixluru .... 1. famous American university

b. neievxpse .... 2. what you wear

c. nyfun .... 3. first meal of the day

d. hsecotl .... 4. costly things that aren't necessary

e. afbkserat .... 5. costs a lot of money

f. lyea............................ 6. makes you laugh

3 Tick (✔) the words that refer to Harris's eating place.

☐ clean   ☐ simple   ☐ famous

☐ good meal   ☐ noisy   ☐ dirty

☐ serves breakfast   ☐ had new customers

T: GRADE 2

4 Topic – Celebrations

Find a photo of a celebration, or an advertisement or a menu for an eating place you know. Think about the following questions:

a. Why did you go to this eating place?

b. Who did you go with?

c. What did you have to eat?

d. Why is this eating place good for a celebration?

MONEY AND ITS ORIGINS

 Long ago there was no money. Banknotes and coins didn't exist. People used all kinds of things as money: food, salt, shells, [1] jewelry, precious metals, cloth, animals. They traded these things for something else. This kind of trading is called barter. [2] Some primitive [3] people still use the barter system. One of the greatest barters in history is the following: In 1626, Peter Minuit, of the Dutch West India Company, bought Manhattan Island (New York) from the Indians. He paid for it with beads and trinkets [4] worth $ 24!

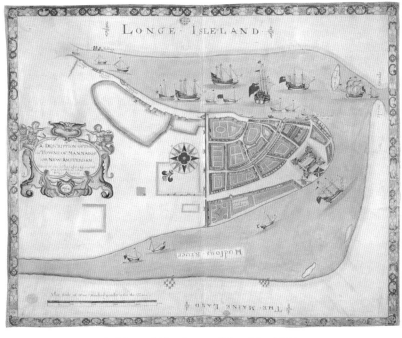

A Map of Manhattan Island in 1664.

1. **shells** :

2. **barter** : trade by exchanging goods for other goods without using money.

3. **primitive** : of or at an early stage of social development.

4. **beads and trinkets** :

65

As time went on, people began to use coins made of gold, silver, copper [1] and other metals. Each country had its own coins of different sizes and shapes.

Until the 1920s banknotes were backed [2] by gold. This was called the "gold standard". [3] It meant that when a person went to the bank and presented a banknote, the bank gave the person the same amount in gold. This is why the words "promise to pay" appeared on banknotes.

Today, coins and banknotes are made in a place called a mint. Banknotes are made with very special paper. This makes it extremely difficult for counterfeiters, people who print their own money, to copy the banknotes. It is against [4] the law, in all countries, to counterfeit money. [5]

Old gold and silver coins.

1. **copper** : a soft, red metal.
2. **backed** : (here) guaranteed.
3. **standard** : how good somebody or something is.
4. **against** : in opposition to.
5. **counterfeit money** : copy or imitate money in order to deceive.

PET **1** Decide if each sentence is correct or incorrect. If it is correct, tick (✓) A; if it is incorrect, tick (✓) B.

	A	B
1. Long ago people used only jewelry and precious metals as money.	☐	☐
2. Trading one thing for something else is called barter.	☐	☐
3. Peter Minuit bought Manhattan Island (New York) from the Indians for $ 24 worth of beads and trinkets.	☐	☐
4. Before 1920 all coins were made of silver.	☐	☐
5. The "gold standard" meant that only gold coins were used in a country.	☐	☐
6. A mint is a place where banknotes are kept.	☐	☐
7. Counterfeiters are people who print their own money.	☐	☐

2 What is the currency of your country?

....

T: GRADE 2

3 Topic – Money
Find some coins or banknotes, if possible from another country. Think about the following questions:

a. What is the name of the currency and how much is it worth in Euros? What could you buy with it in your country?

b. What images or inscription [1] is there?

---

1. **inscription** : words stamped on a coin.

67

Before you read

1 Listen to the first part of Part 6, and then choose the name of the person who said these words.

a. "I think I know you."

- [ ] the American Ambassador
- [ ] Lloyd Hastings
- [ ] Portia Langham

b. "Yes, I'm the strange millionaire with the million-pound note in his pocket!"

- [ ] the narrator
- [ ] the Duke of Shoreditch
- [ ] Lloyd Hastings

c. "Well, well, this *is* a surprise."

- [ ] Lloyd Hastings
- [ ] Henry Adams
- [ ] the American Ambassador

d. "You had a very small salary."

- [ ] Henry Adams
- [ ] Portia Langham
- [ ] Lloyd Hastings

e. "No, no, it was the What Cheer Restaurant."

- [ ] Lloyd Hastings
- [ ] Henry Adams
- [ ] Viscount Cheapside

f. "That night we worked for six long hours on the Gould and Curry Mining Company papers."

- [ ] the American Ambassador
- [ ] Lloyd Hastings
- [ ] Henry Adams

PART 6

The Dinner Party

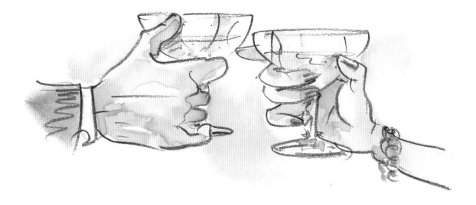

There were fourteen people at the dinner party. The Duke [1] and Duchess [2] of Shoreditch, and their daughter, Lady Anne-Grace-Eleanor de Bohun, the Earl [3] and Countess [4] of Newgate, Viscount [5] Cheapside, Lord and Lady Blatherskite, the Ambassador and his wife and daughter, and some other people. There was also a beautiful, twenty-two-year old English girl, named Portia Langham. I fell in love with her in two minutes, and she with me!

1. **duke** : a nobleman of the highest rank.
2. **duchess** : the wife of a duke.
3. **earl** : a nobleman of high rank.
4. **countess** : the wife of an earl.
5. **viscount** : a nobleman ranking lower than an earl.

After a while, the house servant presented another guest, Mr Lloyd Hastings. When Mr Hastings saw me, he said, "I think I know you."

"Yes, you probably do."

"Are you the — the — "

"Yes, I'm the strange millionaire with the million-pound note in his pocket!"

"Well, well, this *is* a surprise. I never thought you were the same Henry Adams from San Francisco! Six months ago, you were working in the offices of Blake Hopkins in San Francisco. I remember clearly. You had a very small salary. And, at night, you helped me arrange the papers [1] for the Gould and Curry Mining Company. Now you're a millionaire, a celebrity [2] here in London. I can't believe it! How exciting!"

"I can't believe it, either, Lloyd."

"Just three months ago, we went to the Miner's Restaurant — "

"No, no, it was the What Cheer Restaurant."

"Right, it *was* the What Cheer. We went there at two o'clock in the morning. We had steak [3] and coffee. That night we worked for six long hours on the Gould and Curry Mining Company papers. Do you remember, Henry, I asked you to come to London with me. I wanted you to help me sell the Gould and Curry gold mine shares. [4] But you refused."

END

"Of course I remember. I didn't want to leave my job in San Francisco. And, I still think it's difficult to sell shares of a California gold mine here in London."

1. **papers** : official documents.
2. **celebrity** : a famous person.
3. **steak** : a thick piece of meat or fish.
4. **shares** : documents you buy that make you part-owner of a business.

70

"You were right, Henry. You were so right. It is impossible to sell these shares here in London. My plan failed and I spent all my money. I don't want to talk about it."

"But you must talk about it. When we leave the dinner party, you must tell me what happened."

"Oh, can I? I really need to talk to a friend," Lloyd said, with water in his eyes.

"Yes, I want to hear the whole story, every word of it."

"Thank you, Henry. You're a true friend."

At this point, it was time for dinner. Thanks to the English system of precedence, 1 there was no dinner.

---

1.   **precedence** : order to be observed in ceremonies by people of different ranks.

The Duke of Shoreditch wanted to sit at the head of the table. The American Ambassador also wanted to sit at the head of the table. It was impossible for them to decide, so we had no dinner.

The English know about the system of precedence.

They have dinner before going out to dinner. But strangers know nothing about it. They remain hungry all evening.

Instead, we had a dish of sardines [1] and a strawberry. [2] Now it was time for everyone to play a game called cribbage. [3] The English never play a game for fun. They play to win or to lose something.

---

1. **sardines** : small sea-fish.
2. **strawberry** : soft juicy red fruit.
3. **cribbage** : card game.

Miss Langham and I played the game, but with little interest. I looked at her beautiful face and said, "Miss Langham, I love you!"

"Mr Adams," she said softly and smiled, "I love you too!"

This was a wonderful evening. Miss Langham and I were very happy. We smiled, laughed and talked.

I was honest with her. I told her that I was poor and that I didn't have a cent in the world. I explained that the million-pound note was not mine. She was very curious to know more. I told her the whole story from the start. She laughed and laughed. She thought the story was very funny. I didn't understand why it was funny. I also explained that I needed an important job with a big salary to pay all my debts. [1]

"Portia, dear, can you come with me on the day I must meet those two gentlemen?

"Well, yes, if I can help you," she replied.

"Of course you can help me. You are so lovely that when the two gentlemen see you, I can ask for any job and any salary. With you there, my sweet Portia, the two gentlemen won't refuse me anything."

---

1. **debts** : money that must be paid back.

PET **1** **Read the sentences below. For each question put a tick (✓) in the correct box.**

1. Who wanted to sit at the head of the table?
   A ☐ Lloyd Hastings and the Duke of Shoreditch
   B ☐ The American Ambassador and Viscount Cheapside
   C ☐ The American Ambassador and the Duke of Shoreditch
   D ☐ The American Ambassador and Henry Adams

2. Lloyd Hastings worked for
   A ☐ the American the Ambassador
   B ☐ the Gould and Curry Mining Company
   C ☐ Blake Hopkins
   D ☐ Lord Blatherskite

3. In San Francisco, Henry and Lloyd had dinner at
   A ☐ the What Cheer Restaurant
   B ☐ Harris's
   C ☐ the Miner's Restaurant
   D ☐ at home

4. Lloyd Hastings came to London to sell
   A ☐ a San Francisco gold mine
   B ☐ a Nevada gold mine
   C ☐ gold
   D ☐ shares of a California mine

5. There was no dinner at the dinner party, but everyone
   A ☐ danced
   B ☐ listened to music
   C ☐ had a dish of sardines and a strawberry
   D ☐ read the newspaper

6. Portia thought Henry's story was
   A ☐ funny
   B ☐ curious
   C ☐ interesting
   D ☐ sad

75

2 **In Part 6 we see these sentences:**

I remember **clearly***.*
"Mr Adams," she said **softly** *and smiled, "I love you too!"*
Clearly and *softly* are adverbs.
Adverbs describe verbs, other adverbs or adjectives.
Adverbs answer questions such as: *how? when? where?*

Look at these examples:
He spoke **calmly***.* (*calmly* describes how he spoke)
She went to a party **yesterday***.* (*yesterday* describes when she went to the party)
They sat **there***.* (*there* describes where they sat)

Fill in the gaps with the correct adverb from the box.

> **tomorrow   here   suddenly   slowly and carefully**
>
> **today   quickly   well**

a. He will pay for the suit ....

b. ...., he became famous.

c. Henry Adams met the Ambassador ....

d. "Please sit ....," said Lloyd.

e. We ran .... across the street.

f. Henry read the letter ....

g. We didn't feel .... after the dinner.

LONDON TODAY

London today covers 100 square miles, with a population of about 7,000,000 people. It is one of Europe's most interesting capitals. The nation's government is the Parliament, at Westminster. In the clock tower near the House of Commons, is London's famous time-keeper, [1] Big Ben.

The Houses of Parliament.

Magnificent [2] Westminster Abbey is nearby. It was built in the 11th century by King Edward the Confessor. [3] Many of England's kings and queens were crowned here.

---

1. **time-keeper** : (here) clock.
2. **magnificent** : very good or beautiful.
3. **confessor** : priest who hears confessions.

Buckingham Palace.

Buckingham Palace is the Queen's impressive [1] London home. In front of the Palace, visitors can enjoy the ceremony of the Changing of the Guard. It takes place at 11.30 am daily in the summer, and on alternate days in the winter.

Trafalgar Square, with Nelson's Column, is a busy place. The National Gallery [2] is at Trafalgar Square. It has one of the best collections of European paintings from the 13th century to the 1900s.

The Changing of the Guard.

1. **impressive** : making somebody have good feelings.
2. **gallery** : a building for showing works of art.

Going east along the River Thames, there is the famous Tower of London and the 19th-century Tower Bridge. The White Tower is the oldest part of the Tower of London. It was built by William the Conqueror in 1078. The Crown Jewels are kept in the Jewel House.

Tower Bridge.

There are several beautiful parks to visit in London: Hyde Park, Kensington Gardens, St James's Park, Battersea Park and Regent's Park with its zoo.

The area from Kensington Gardens to Cromwell Road is "museumland". The Science Museum, Natural History Museum, Geological Museum, and Victoria and Albert Museum are in South Kensington. The British Museum, one of the greatest museums of the world, is in the district of Bloomsbury.

London is a wonderful place to shop. The variety [1] of things to

1. **variety** : number or range of different things.

buy is huge. In the West End, London's most fashionable shopping streets are Oxford Street, Regent Street and Bond Street. There are a lot of fine shops and department stores in the area of Piccadilly Circus.

Kensington High Street and King's Road are good shopping areas for young fashions. [1]

Knightsbridge is the home of Harrods, London's most famous department store.

Covent Garden is near Charing Cross. It was once a fruit and vegetable market. Now it is a covered shopping area, with elegant restaurants, bars, shops and street entertainers. [2]

Covent Garden.

Harrod's Department Store.

London has an excellent underground public transportation system, called the tube. It takes people to all parts of London rapidly.

1. **fashions** : popular styles of clothes or behaviour.
2. **entertainers** : people who make others have a good time.

1 Can you find your way around London? Try this crossword puzzle.

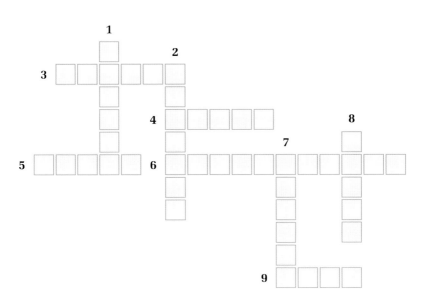

Down

1. Buckingham ....
2. Cathedral in the City
7. Men who protect the palace
8. The King's wife

Across

3. London's River
4. Green areas in London
5. Tall, thin building
6. Runs under London
9. Place where you buy things

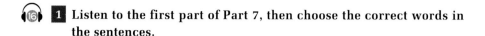

Before you read

1 **Listen to the first part of Part 7, then choose the correct words in the sentences.**

a. At the *and/end* of the dinner *party/part*, I returned to the *house/hotel* with Hastings.

b. *She/He* talked about his *problems/projects*.

c. I was thinking about *Portland Place/Portia* the *hole/whole* time.

d. When *he/we* arrived at the *hostel/hotel*, Hastings said, "Let me just *stand/stay* here and look at this *magnificent/marvelous* hotel."

e. What *expensive/extensive* furniture!

f. You have *anything/everything* you *want/wish*.

g. I, *too/two*, was poor.

h. This was my *latest/last* hope.

i. Do you want to *hear/here* my story?

j. Is *someone/something* wrong with you?

Now read the first three paragraphs and check your answers.

PART 7

A Million-Dollar Idea

At the end of the dinner party, I returned to the hotel with Hastings. He talked about his problems, but I didn't listen to him. I was thinking about Portia the whole time.

When we arrived at the hotel, Hastings said, "Let me just stand here and look at this marvelous [1] hotel. It's a palace! What expensive furniture! You have everything you want. You are rich, Henry. And I am poor."

His words scared [2] me. I, too, was poor. I didn't have a cent in the world, and I had debts to pay. I needed to win the gentleman's bet. This was my last hope. Hastings didn't know the truth.

"Henry, just a tiny part of your income can save me. I'm

---

1. **marvelous** : very good.　　　2. **scared** : made afraid.

desperate!" Hastings cried.

"My dear Hastings, sit down here and drink this hot whiskey. Now tell me your whole story, every word of it."

"Do you want to hear my story again?"

"But, you never told me your story."

"Of course I told you my story, as we walked to the hotel. Don't you remember?"

"I didn't hear one word of it."

"Henry, are you ill? Is something wrong with you? What did you drink at the dinner party?"

"Oh, Hastings, I'm in love! I can only think about my sweet

Portia. This is why I didn't hear your story before."

Hastings got up from his chair, shook my hand [1] and laughed.

"I'm very happy for you, Henry, very happy," he said smiling. "I'll tell you the whole story again." So he sat down and patiently started to tell me his story.

To make a long story short, [2] the owners of the Gould and Curry Gold Mine sent Lloyd to England, to sell the shares of

1. **shook my hand** : held my hand and moved it up and down.
2. **to make a long story short** : briefly, in short.

the mine for one million dollars. Any money he received over one million dollars was his to keep. Hastings's dream was to sell the shares for more than one million dollars, and become rich. He had only one month to sell the shares. He had done everything to sell them, but nobody wanted to buy them.

Then he jumped up and cried, "Henry, you can help me! Will you do it?"

"Tell me how."

"Give me a million dollars and I'll sell you all the shares. You will be the new owner of the gold mine. Don't, don't refuse."

I did not know what to say. I wanted to tell Hastings the truth. But then, an intelligent idea came to me. I thought about it for a moment and then calmly said, "I will save you, Lloyd."

"Then I am already saved! How can I thank you — "

"Let me finish, Lloyd. I will save you, but not in that way. I have a better way. I know everything about that mine. I know its great value. You will sell the shares by *using my name*. You can send anyone to me, since people in London know me. I will guarantee [1] the gold mine. In a week or two, you will sell the shares for three million dollars, by using my name. And we'll share [2] the money you earn. Half to you and half to me."

Lloyd was very happy and excited. He danced around the room and laughed.

"I can use your name! Your name — think of it. The rich Londoners will run to buy these shares. I'm saved! And I'll never forget you, Henry!"

1.   **guarantee** : promise to be legally responsible for.
2.   **share** : divide.

1 **What happened in Part 7?**

  a. Why didn't Henry listen to Lloyd's problems?

  b. Where did Henry and Lloyd go after the dinner party?

  c. What was Lloyd's dream?

  d. How did Lloyd ask Henry to help him?

  e. How will Henry help Lloyd to sell the shares?

2 **What do you know about the people in the story? Match the characters with the information below. Put the letters a-h in the correct boxes.**

  a. Henry Adams   **1.** ☐ works in a tailor's shop

  b. Two old gentlemen   **2.** ☐ English nobleman

  c. Harris   **3.** ☐ worked for Blake Hopkins

  d. Tod   **4.** ☐ represents the United States of America in England

  e. American Ambassador   **5.** ☐ made an unusual bet

  f. Duke of Shoreditch   **6.** ☐ lovely, young English girl

  g. Lloyd Hastings   **7.** ☐ owns an eating place

  h. Portia Langham   **8.** ☐ wants to sell shares

The Stars and Stripes.

The Union Jack.

PART 8

Back to Portland Place

T he next day, all of London talked about the shares of the California gold mine. I stayed in my hotel and said to everyone who came to me, "Yes, I know Mr Hastings. He's a very honest man. And I know the gold mine, because I lived in the California Gold Country. It is a mine of great value." People were now interested in buying the shares.

I spent every evening with Portia at the American Ambassador's house. I didn't tell her about the shares and the mine. It was a surprise. [1] We talked about our love and our future together.

Finally, the end of the month arrived. Lots of rich Londoners bought the shares of the mine. I had a million

---

1. **surprise** : something that happens unexpectedly.

dollars of my own in the London and County Bank. And Lloyd did too.

It was time to meet with the two old gentlemen. I dressed in my best clothes, and I went to get Portia.

Before going to Portland Place, Portia and I talked about the job and the salary.

"Portia, you are so beautiful! When the two gentlemen meet you, they will give me any job and any salary I ask for."

"Henry, please remember that if we ask for too much, we will get nothing. Then what will happen to us?"

"Don't be afraid, Portia."

When we arrived, the same servant opened the door. There were the two old gentlemen having tea. They were surprised to see Portia. I introduced her to them.

Then I said, "Gentlemen, I am ready to report to you."

"We are pleased to hear this," said one gentleman. "Now we can decide the bet that my brother Abel and I made. If you won for me, you can have any job in my power. Do you have the million-pound note?"

"Here it is, sir," and I gave it to him.

"I won!" he shouted. "Now what do you say, Abel?"

"I say he survived, and I lost twenty thousand pounds. I can't believe it!

"I have more to tell you," I said. "But, it's a long story. I'll tell you another time. For now, look at this."

"What! A Certificate 1 of Deposit 2 for £ 200,000. Is it yours?"

"It's mine. I earned it by using the banknote you lent me for a month."

"This is astonishing! 3 I can't believe it."

Portia looked at me with surprise and said, "Henry, is that really your money? You didn't tell me the truth."

---

1. **certificate** : an important piece of paper that shows something is true.
2. **deposit** : money that you pay into a bank.
3. **astonishing** : very surprising.

"No, I didn't. But, I know you'll forgive [1] me."

"Don't be so sure! You told me a lie, Henry."

"Dearest Portia, it was only for fun. Come, let's go now."

"But, wait, wait!" my gentleman said. "I want to give you the job and the salary you choose."

"Thank you, thank you with all my heart. But I don't want the job."

"Henry, you didn't thank the good gentleman in the right way. Can I do it for you?" Portia said.

"Of course you can, my dear."

Portia walked to my gentleman, sat on his lap [2] and kissed him on the mouth.

Then the two old gentlemen shouted and laughed. I was amazed. [3] What was happening?

"Papa," said Portia, "Henry doesn't want your job. I feel very hurt."

"Darling, is that your father?" I asked.

"Yes, he's my stepfather, [4] a dear man. Now do you understand why I laughed when you told me your story?"

"My dearest sir," I said, "I want to take back [5] what I said. There *is* a job that I want."

"Tell me!"

"I want the job of son-in-law." [6]

---

1. **forgive** : say that you are no longer angry with someone.
2. **lap** : (here) knees.
3. **amazed** : surprised.
4. **stepfather** : the husband of Portia's mother, not her real father.
5. **take back** : change what I said before.
6. **son-in-law** : husband of the daughter.

"Well, well, well. But you were never a son-in-law before. Do you know how to do this job?"

"Try me, please! Try me for thirty or forty years, and if — "

"Oh, all right. Take her!"

Were Portia and I happy? There aren't enough words in the dictionary to describe our happiness. When the Londoners heard the whole story of my adventures with the banknote, they talked of nothing else.

Portia's father took the banknote back to the Bank of England and cashed [1] it. Then he gave us the cancelled banknote [2] as a wedding present. We put it in a picture frame [3] and hung it on the wall in our new home.

And so I always say, "Yes, it's a million-pound banknote, but it only bought one thing in its life: the most valuable [4] thing in the world — Portia!"

---

1. **cashed** : changed into real money.
2. **the cancelled banknote** : the banknote that cannot be used again.
3. **picture frame** :
4. **valuable** : worth a lot of money.

1 **What happened in Part 8?**

a. What did Henry tell the people who were interested in the gold mine?

b. How much money did Henry and Lloyd make by selling the shares?

c. Who lost the bet and how much did he lose?

d. Why was Henry amazed?

e. What job did Henry finally want?

f. Where did Henry and Portia put the million-pound banknote?

2 *Mine, yours, his, hers, ours, theirs* **are possessive pronouns**（物主代詞）**. Fill in the gaps with the correct possessive pronoun.**

a. "Is this their home?" asked Lloyd. "Yes, it's ....," answered Henry.

b. "I forgot my umbrella. Lend me ...., please," said Portia to Henry.

c. "That's Abel's money. Don't touch it. It's ...."

d. "He's got his coat, but where is (Portia) ....?"

e. "This beautiful picture frame is ....," said Henry and Portia.

f. "Is this your £ 1,000,000 banknote?" asked Harris. "Yes, it's ....," answered Henry.

3 If you found a £ 1,000,000 banknote, what would you do and why? (You can choose more than one answer.)

a. ☐ give it to the police
b. ☐ keep it and save it
c. ☐ keep it and spend it
d. ☐ tell your friends
e. ☐ tell your parents
f. ☐ tell no one
g. ☐ give it away to charity

4 After finding the £ 1,000,000 banknote, and deciding what to do with it, how would you feel and why?

a. ☐ nervous
b. ☐ happy
c. ☐ worried
d. ☐ excited
e. ☐ unhappy
f. ☐ guilty
g. ☐ honest

5 If you decided to keep it and spend it, what is the first thing you would buy?

....
....
....

THE ORIGINS OF BANKING

Banking first appeared in Babylon in the year 1,000 BC in the form of safekeeping [1] lending and transfers. [2] Banking also developed in Greece in the year 700 BC, and in Egypt in the year 400 BC.

Modern banking, as we know it today, began with Italian merchants and London goldsmiths, [3] who gave credit to depositors. [4] Between the 12th and the 15th centuries, Italy was Europe's most important financial and commercial power. In the 12th century, the banks of Genoa accepted deposits and exchanged foreign coins for local currency. Later, the Florentines became the leading Italian bankers.

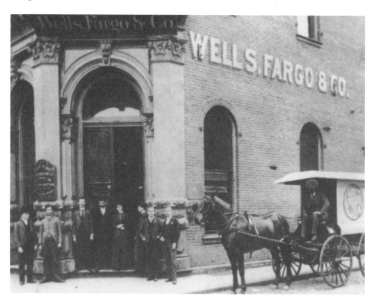

The first important bank in San Francisco.

1. **safekeeping** : protecting money or objects of value.
2. **transfers** : moving something from one place to another.
3. **goldsmiths** : people who make things out of gold.
4. **depositors** : people who put money in a bank.

The Medici Family of Florence was the greatest of all 15th-century Italian bankers. They had offices in France, England, the Netherlands and throughout Italy. As time went on, banks developed all over Europe and in the New World.

1 Tick (✓) the correct answer.

a. Banking first appeared in
- [ ] Italy
- [ ] Babylon
- [ ] Greece

b. Banking as we know it today began with
- [ ] Egyptian merchants
- [ ] Greek merchants
- [ ] Italian merchants and London goldsmiths

c. Europe's most important financial and commercial power between the 12th and 15th centuries was
- [ ] Italy
- [ ] England
- [ ] Florence

d. In the 12th century, the banks of Genoa
- [ ] were very small
- [ ] had offices throughout Italy
- [ ] accepted deposits and exchanged foreign coins

e. In the 15th century, the greatest Italian bankers were
- [ ] the Medici Family of Florence
- [ ] the families of Genoa
- [ ] the goldsmiths of Florence

EXIT TEST

1 Can you make a summary of the story? Put these sentences in the correct order. Write 1, 2, 3 etc. in the boxes. One is done for you.

a ☐ I agreed to help Lloyd to sell the shares by using my name.

b ☐ When I returned to the two gentlemen's house, they had gone to the Continent.

c ☐ The two gentlemen gave me an envelope with money and a letter inside.

d ☐ At the end of the month, I returned to the two gentlemen's house and showed them the million-pound note.

e ☐ The owner of the eating place apologized because he was not able to change the banknote.

f ☐ Lloyd asked me to help him sell the shares of a California Gold Mine.

g ☐ When I arrived in London, I had only one dollar in my pocket.

h ☐ The owner of the tailor's ordered his tailors to make me suits, shirts and coats.

i ☐ When I opened the envelope and saw the million-pound banknote, I almost fainted.

j ☐ I had won the bet for the old gentleman, and I asked him for the job of son-in-law.

k ☐ At Portland Place, two gentlemen made a bet, and I was the right man for the bet.

l 1 One Saturday afternoon I sailed out too far, and the strong wind blew my sailboat into the Pacific Ocean.

m ☐ He thought I was a rich gentleman who liked playing jokes on people by dressing like a poor man.

n ☐ At a dinner party, I met Portia Langham and Lloyd Hastings.

o ☐ Lots of rich Londoners bought the shares of the gold mine, and Lloyd and I became rich.

2 What other English words about money do you know?
Make a spidergram like this:

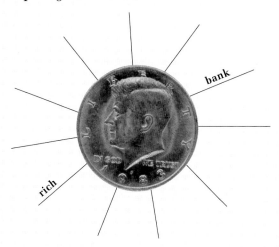

3 Write a "book report" of this story.

Title 1 ....

Author 2 ....

Characters   main 3 ....

minor 4 ....

Setting   place(s) 5 ....

time 6 ....

Short summary

This book is about 7 ....

....

....

4 A journalist from *Punch* magazine interviews Henry Adams.
Read this interview with Henry Adams, and then fill in the blank
spaces using the words from the box.

> horse   bought   rode   countryside   everything   strange
> follow   British   twenty-seven   weeks   humor   people
> famous   spend   buy   American   beautiful

Interviewer: How old are you, Mr Adams?

Henry Adams: I'm 1......................... years old.

Interviewer: How long have you been in London?

Henry Adams: Oh, I've been here about five 2......................... .

Interviewer: Do you know that you're the most 3.........................
person in London at the moment?

Henry Adams: Well, yes, I've noticed that 4......................... look at
me, and 5......................... me around town.

Interviewer: People say that you're a 6......................... millionaire.
Are you?

Henry Adams: Yes, I think I am! I am able to buy 7.........................
I want by showing my million-pound note.

Interviewer: What have you 8......................... recently?

Henry Adams: I've always wanted a fast 9........................., and
yesterday I found a 10......................... black horse that I liked. I
examined him carefully. I 11......................... him for a few kilometers
in the 12......................... . He was very fast and jumped fences well.
So, I decided to 13......................... him.

Interviewer: How much did you 14.........................?

Henry Adams: Ah, that's a secret!

Interviewer: You're an 15........................., Mr Adams. What do you
like best about the 16.........................?

Henry Adams: I love their sense of 17........................., and I love their
beautiful girls!

Score

100

The £ 1,000,000 Bank Note

KEY TO
THE ACTIVITIES
AND EXIT TEST

KEY TO THE ACTIVITIES

SAN FRANCISCO IN THE 1850s

Page 13 exercises 1-2
1. A
2. B – At the beginning of the 1800s, there were few ships in the bay.
3. A
4. B – In only one year, its population went from 1,000 to 30,000.
5. A
6. B – In the 1850s San Francisco was the most important city on the Pacific Coast.
7. B – This story begins in San Francisco.

Page 14 – Before you read
a. 2 / b. 3 / c. 6 / d. 4 / e. 1 / f. 5

Part 1

Page 20 exercise 1
a. In San Francisco.
b. It pushed it out of the bay, into the Pacific Ocean.
c. On a British brig.
d. Because he was very hungry.

e. Discussing something important.

Page 20 exercise 2
1. c / 2. a / 3. b / 4. c / 5. b or d / 6. c

SAILING SHIPS

Page 23
a. Egyptian ships / b. oars / c. China / d. clipper / e. San Francisco / f. brig

SAILING ON SAN FRANCISCO BAY

Page 26 exercise 1
a. 5 / b. 6 / c. 2 / d. 3 / e. 4 / f. 1

Page 26 exercise 2

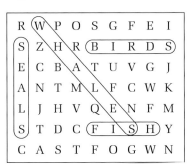

Part 2

Page 35 exercise 1

a. Brother A said, "If an honest and intelligent stranger arrives in London without a friend and without money, except for the £ 1,000,000 bank note, he will starve to death." Brother B said, "No, he didn't."

b. That a stranger will live for 30 days with the bank note and not go to prison.

c. £ 20,000.

d. Because he was a stranger and seemed honest, intelligent and poor.

e. A letter and a £ 1,000,000 bank note.

f. Because he could not change the bank note.

Page 35 exercise 2

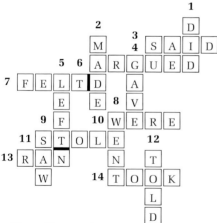

Page 36 exercise 3

a. is / will be   b. rains / won't go

c. opens / will find   d. will win / follow
e. will push / sail   f. will be / work

THE ENGLISH AND BETTING

Page 38 exercise 1

a. B – The British love betting.
b. A
c. B – A lot of betting takes place at the pub.
d. A
e. A
f. B – Las Vegas is a town in the state of Nevada.

Page 39 – Before you read

1. B – He hurried to the house of the two gentlemen.
2. B – The two gentlemen went to the Continent.
3. A
4. B – The family went to Egypt and India.
5. B – There was no signature on the letter.
6. A
7. A
8. B – The narrator decided to keep the bill for a month.
9. A

Part 3

Page 44 exercise 1

a. To correct the mistake the two gentlemen had made.
b. To the Continent.
c. "You are an intelligent and honest man. You are also poor and a stranger. In this envelope you will find some money. It is yours only for 30 days. At the end of 30 days, return to this house. I have a bet on

you. If I win this bet, you can have any job with any salary that you want."

d. Because the bank would ask him lots of questions.

e. He planned to keep the bill for a month.

f. The idea of an important job with a big salary.

Page 45 exercise 3

a. You mustn't enter this property.
b. You mustn't walk on the grass.
c. You mustn't take dogs inside.
d. You mustn't talk.
e. You must fasten your seatbelts.
f. You must pay / buy your ticket here.
g. You mustn't enter./You mustn't light a fire here.

LONDINIUM

Page 48 exercise 1

a. St Paul's Cathedral, the Barbican, Museum of London.

b. 3 – Hyde Park, Regent's Park, Green Park.

c. 7 – Natural History Museum, Science Museum, Victoria and Albert Museum, British Museum, Museum of London, Geffrye Museum, Imperial War Museum.

d. 3 – The National Film, National Theatre, Royal Opera House.

e. The Serpentine.

Page 49 – Before you read

1. C / **2.** A / **3.** B / **4.** A / **5.** B / **6.** C

Part 4

Page 55 exercise 1

1. B / **2.** A / **3.** C / **4.** D / **5.** B / **6.** C
7. A / **8.** C / **9.** A

Page 55 exercise 2

a. 7 / **b.** 4 / **c.** 1 / **d.** 8 / **e.** 2 / **f.** 5 / **g.** 3 / **h.** 6

Page 56 exercise 3

a. poorer / poorest **b.** colder / coldest
c. cheaper /cheapest **d.** happier / happiest **e.** kinder / kindest
f. bigger / biggest

HOW DID PEOPLE DRESS IN THE 1850s?

Page 58

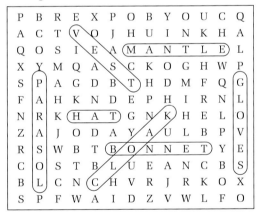

Page 59 – Before you read

1. A
2. B – No one was able to change the bank note.
3. B – He stayed at an expensive hotel in Hanover Square.

4. A
5. B – He preferred having breakfast at Harris's.
6. A
7. A
8. A
9. B – He sometimes wore them.
10. B – He knew the narrator's father from Yale University.

Part 5

Page 63 exercise 1
1. D / 2. C / 3. B / 4. D / 5. B

Page 64 exercise 2
a. luxuries (4) / **b.** expensive (5) /
c. funny (6) / **d.** clothes (2) /
e. breakfast (3) / **f.** Yale (1)

Page 64 exercise 3
famous, serves breakfast, simple, good meal, had new customers

MONEY AND ITS ORIGINS

Page 67 exercise 1
1. B – People used all kinds of things as money.
2. A
3. A
4. B – Coins were made of gold, silver, copper and other metals.
5. B – It meant that when a person went to the bank and presented a bank note, the bank gave the person the same amount in gold.
6. B – A mint is a place where bank notes are made.
7. A

Page 68 – Before you read
a. Lloyd Hastings
b. the narrator
c. Lloyd Hastings
d. Lloyd Hastings
e. Henry Adams
f. Lloyd Hastings

Part 6

Page 75 exercise 1
1. C / 2. C / 3. A / 4. D / 5. C / 6. A

Page 76 exercise 2
a. tomorrow
b. Suddenly
c. today
d. here
e. quickly
f. slowly and carefully
g. well

LONDON TODAY

Page 81

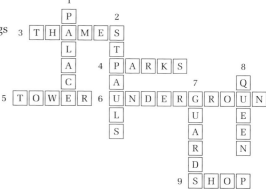

Page 82 – Before you read
a. end / party / hotel

b. He / problems
c. Portia / whole
d. we / hotel / stand / marvellous
e. expensive
f. everything / want
g. too
h. last
i. hear
j. something

Part 7

Page 87 exercise 1

a. He was thinking about Portia.
b. To Henry's hotel.
c. To sell the shares for more than one million dollars and become rich.
d. He asked Henry to buy the gold mine for one million dollars.
e. Lloyd can use his name, and Henry will guarantee the gold mine.

Page 87 exercise 2

1.d / 2.f / 3.a / 4.e / 5.b / 6.h / 7.c / 8.g

Part 8

Page 94 exercise 1

a. That he knew Mr Hastings, that he was an honest man, that he knew the gold mine, and that it was a mine of great value.
b. Two million dollars.
c. Abel lost £ 20,000.
d. One of the gentlemen was Portia's stepfather.
e. The job of son-in-law.
f. They put it in a picture frame and hung it on the wall.

Page 94 exercise 2

a. theirs **b.** yours **c.** his **d.** hers
e. ours **f.** mine

THE ORIGINS OF BANKING

Page 97 exercise 1

a. Babylon
b. Italian merchants and London goldsmiths
c. Italy
d. accepted deposits and exchanged foreign coins
e. the Medici Family of Florence

KEY TO THE EXIT TEST

Page 98 exercise 1

a. 12 **b.** 8 **c.** 4 **d.** 14 **e.** 6 **f.** 11 **g.** 2
h. 9 **i.** 5 **j.** 15 **k.** 3 **l.** 1 **m.** 7 **n.** 10
o. 13

Page 98 exercises 2-3

Open answers.

Page 100 exercise 4

1. twenty-seven / **2.** weeks / **3.** famous /
4. people / **5.** follow / **6.** strange /
7. everything / **8.** bought / **9.** horse /
10. beautiful / **11.** rode /
12. countryside / **13.** buy / **14.** spend /
15. American / **16.** British / **17.** humor

Notes

Notes

Notes

Notes

Notes

Black Cat English Readers

BLACK CAT ENGLISH CLUB
Membership Application Form

BLACK CAT ENGLISH CLUB is for those who love English reading and seek for better English to share and learn with fun together.

Benefits offered:
- Membership Card
- Member badge, poster, bookmark
- Book discount coupon
- Black Cat English Reward Scheme
- English learning e-forum
- Surprise gift and more...

Simply fill out the application form below and fax it back to 2565 1113.

Join Now! It's **FREE** exclusively for readers who have purchased *Black Cat English Readers* !

The book(or book set) that you have purchased: _____

English Name:_____ (Surname) _____ (Given Name)

Chinese Name: _____

Address:_____

Tel: _____ Fax: _____

Email:_____
(Login password for e-forum will be sent to this email address.)

Sex: ❑ Male   ❑ Female

Education Background: ❑ Primary 1-3   ❑ Primary 4-6   ❑ Junior Secondary Education (F1-3)
                     ❑ Senior Secondary Education (F4-5)   ❑ Matriculation
                     ❑ College   ❑ University or above

Age: ❑ 6 - 9   ❑ 10 - 12   ❑ 13 - 15   ❑ 16 - 18   ❑ 19 - 24   ❑ 25 - 34
     ❑ 35 - 44   ❑ 45 - 54   ❑ 55 or above

Occupation: ❑ Student   ❑ Teacher   ❑ White Collar   ❑ Blue Collar
             ❑ Professional   ❑ Manager   ❑ Business Owner   ❑ Housewife
             ❑ Others (please specify: _____)

As a member, what would you like **BLACK CAT ENGLISH CLUB** to offer:
   ❑ Member gathering/ party   ❑ English class with native teacher   ❑ English competition
   ❑ Newsletter   ❑ Online sharing   ❑ Book fair
   ❑ Book discount   ❑ Others (please specify: _____)

Other suggestions to **BLACK CAT ENGLISH CLUB**:

_____

Please sign here: _____

(Date:_____)